UXB: Unexploded Bomb

Written by John Parsons
Illustrated by Scott Fraser

Contents

For learning solutions, visit **cengage.com.au**

Meet the Characters

"Chalkie" Sykes

A British Mosquito pilot.

"Mac" McPherson

A British Mosquito navigator.

Monique

A brave resident of St Augiére.

Sebastian

Monique's father.

Roland

Monique's brother.

Jean-Claude

A bomb disposal expert.

Dear Reader

During World War II (1939–45), hundreds of thousands of bombs rained down on Europe. Many did not explode and lay buried beneath the soil. They are called UXBs, or unexploded bombs. I wanted to write a story about two UXBs – one, a real bomb that is discovered, and the other, a long-forgotten secret of betrayal!

John Parsons
Author

St Augiére in 1943

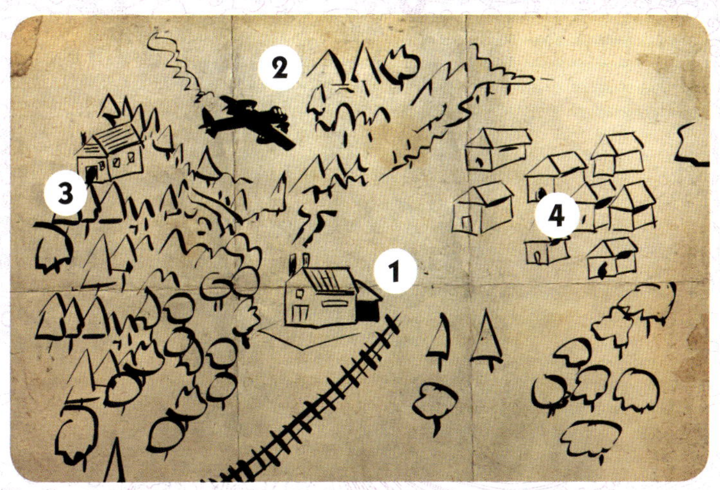

1. The workshop
2. The crash site
3. The farmhouse
4. St Augiére

1 Dangerous Times

1943. Dangerous times. The full moon broke through the cloud cover, and a rippling slick of molten silver seemed to flash across the vast expanse of the Bay of Biscay. At 350 kilometres per hour, barely ten metres above the choppy waves, the Mosquito bomber tore through the night sky, its twin engines roaring.

The Mosquito's pilot, Squadron Leader Sykes, was nicknamed "Chalkie" because of his wild shock of blond hair. To the west, he saw nothing through the cockpit windshield except black sea. A low sea fog blurred the line between sea and sky to the east, and beyond that lay occupied France.

Behind him, Chalkie's navigator, Ian "Mac" McPherson, checked his wristwatch. He distilled time, airspeed and revised direction into a thin pencil line on his navigational chart.

Chalkie flicked a switch to jettison the tanks and, freed of the extra air resistance, the Mosquito's nose rose slightly. Chalkie levelled the aircraft out, knowing that if they flew above thirty metres and were detected, German fighter planes would be scrambled from their bases along western France.

"There!" shouted Mac.

At once, Chalkie saw the black outlines of the mountains looming through the fog.

Mac flicked his eyes between the dark mountains and the relief map on his knees, urgently trying to match the two.

"Keep tracking north," he said, the calmness in his voice disguising his rising anxiety. His suspicions had proven correct. Their long journey, keeping a safe distance from the French coast, had taken them fifty kilometres south of where they should have been. That meant retracing their path. If enemy troops along the coast had heard the roar of their engines, they'd alert the anti-aircraft guns to the north.

"Tracking north," confirmed Chalkie. He knew the danger they faced, but there was no turning back.

They'd come this far, and the mission had to be completed. If they survived, they'd have two long hours to worry about getting home, but right now, he needed to concentrate on reaching the target.

1985. Bewildering times. Ten years ago, retirement had seemed like a good idea – long days to fill with hobbies or pottering in the garden shed. But now that it had finally arrived, retirement had quickly become boring. For years, there had always been a reason to get up in the mornings and now, suddenly, there was none.

The man stretched his aching leg as far as he could into the aisle of the train carriage. It had been a long journey back to London after his visit north to see an old friend. He rattled the pages of his newspaper and glanced at the headlines. Then he spotted it: a short paragraph buried in the overseas news on page eleven. It was curious how, in a page of text, the eyes could be drawn immediately to a word, a place name or a face that one immediately recognised. Suddenly, the ache in the man's leg vanished as he fixed his attention on the tiny article. He no longer heard the clatter of the carriage on the tracks, the chatter of the other passengers, the whoosh of brick walls and station platforms as they sped past. He stared at the photo accompanying the article. Those eyes. Cold, grey, expressionless.

2 Fate Approaches

Sebastian quietly closed the door of the wooden house nestled amongst the fir trees, so as not to wake his daughter, Monique, and hurried to catch up with his son, Roland. The rough track leading down the mountainside demanded caution, even in the daylight, but there was little time for extra care.

The Germans who controlled the engineering workshop where they were forced to work had no time for excuses. If you were late, the best you could hope for was to have your rations cut for a week. The worst did not bear thinking about. That week, they'd demanded the workforce turn up half an hour earlier than before. Sebastian, Roland and the other hundred workers had no choice but to arrive for work before sunrise and return home exhausted after nightfall.

Father and son picked their way through the woods and came to a road. Each morning, before dawn, the routine was the same. Hurry to the workshop, sign in, and then work as slowly as they could without

Hurry up! Soon the sun will rise and we'll be in trouble.
We'll make, it Roland. I don't know why you're so keen to help the Germans.
Things are the way they are. The Germans are here, and we might as well make the best of it.

attracting the Germans' attention. Every hour that they and the rest of the conscripted workforce delayed repairs to the tanks and armoured vehicles crowded into the workshop meant another hour those tanks and vehicles could not patrol the roads of occupied France.

"Hurry up," hissed Roland, striding along the road. "Soon the sun will rise and we'll be in trouble."

"We'll make, it Roland," replied Sebastian. He looked at his wristwatch. "I don't know why you're so keen to help the Germans. I can almost smell the acorn coffee they make us drink instead of the real thing."

"Things are the way they are," muttered Roland. "The Germans are here, and we might as well make the best of it."

Five minutes later, they hurried through the town of St Augiére. Eyes down, they ignored the grey-uniformed soldiers milling around the three camouflaged anti-aircraft guns, drinking real coffee. Sebastian and Roland headed for the heavy steel doors of the workshop.

Mac had pinpointed their position. “Another two minutes,” he called. “We’re hugging the coastline, so we’ll need a sharp roll starboard. The valley’s very narrow. If we overshoot at this altitude, we won’t have time to climb out of trouble.”

Chalkie nodded. He’d have preferred to fly straight into the valley, its soaring cliff faces safely to either side of his wings. But night navigation was imperfect, and they’d make do. He started counting down in his head. The pair of massive 450-kilogram high-explosive bombs the Mosquito carried beneath its wings would make the aircraft sluggish in a tight turn and he needed to be ready the instant he spotted the gap in the mountains.

“Thirty seconds,” came Mac’s voice.

Twenty seconds out, the first rays of the morning sun revealed a finger of fog extending inland between the mountains.

“Bingo,” murmured Chalkie, pulling the nose of the Mosquito upwards and rolling the aircraft over. The bomber banked steeply and Chalkie executed a tight 90-degree turn.

He pushed the throttle full forward and the Mosquito surged towards its target. "Here comes your wake-up call," murmured Chalkie, as the aircraft skimmed above the valley floor, soaring cliffs speeding past on either side.

The train passenger read the paragraph again and again, as if he was reading another story in between the stark words in front of him. He'd just spent the previous evening talking about this very place, both he and his friend shaking their heads and thinking of long-distant events in a world that no longer existed.

He read the article again. Then he folded the newspaper and stared out the window. The landscape flashed by at high speed, rolling countryside, dotted with farmhouses and neat paddocks. But the landscape that the man saw in his memory was quite different – dark and mountainous, forbidding and dangerous. It, too, flashed by at high speed and, as the carriage rocked and swayed, the man was transported back through the years to another time and place.

3 A Split-Second Decision

Even at top speed, the roar of the Mosquito's engines reached the ears of the German troops thirty seconds before they saw the tiny speck thundering straight towards them.

A second later, the harrowing scream of an air-raid siren split the silent dawn air, and the German troops raced to their positions. The anti-aircraft gunners swivelled the three eighty-eight-millimetre cannons westwards, directly down the valley, while armourers feverishly loaded explosive shells into the breeches.

Other troops raced to their positions alongside the workshop, their weapons pointing skywards. Inside, the siren caused pandemonium. German guards barked orders and the workers ran for the door. Everyone knew that the ear-splitting sound meant within seconds they – and the German tanks – would be in the crosshairs of a bomb guide. The workers had arrived minutes beforehand – now they had only desperate seconds to escape.

The Mosquito powered towards the target, its long, curved wings skirting the valley floor. Chalkie's focus was on the building in front of him. Flying near the limits of its capabilities, the aircraft started to shudder and weave imperceptibly and Chalkie forced himself to hold the Mosquito steady.

"Fuses armed!" called Mac. Hours before, the bomb loaders had fitted delayed detonation fuses into the 450-kilogram bombs, because they'd known the mission called for a low-altitude attack. If a bomb detonated on impact, the blast of high explosive might destroy the aircraft.

A slow, curving line of white lights rose from one of the machine guns by the workshop and, as Chalkie sped closer, they shot past like glowing, white-hot balls of lightning. Tracer. Every fifth bullet from the machine gun was a bullet that burned as it sped towards its target, helping the gunners to see exactly where they were firing – and correct their aim.

"Fire!" shouted the soldier in command of the anti-aircraft guns. Three piercing booms echoed through St Augiére as each cannon unleashed a shell towards the oncoming attacker. Two black smudges appeared to the left of the aircraft, then a third burst to its right.

"Too short," yelled the anti-aircraft commander. "Adjust your firing!"

Within seconds, the armourers reloaded the guns and another burst of shells was fired.

CRACK!

Chalkie felt the Mosquito judder as an explosion sent it reeling towards the starboard and fragments of deadly shrapnel tore through its wings.

"That was close," he said, using all his strength to manoeuvre the aircraft back to a level angle.

Inside the workshop, there was a desperate crush as men tried to push their way through the steel doors. The Germans refused to open the doors wide enough to let more than two or three men past at a time, fearing a nearby explosion could blast inside the workshop and damage the tanks there. Sebastian and Roland shouted at the men in front of them.

"Hurry up," they bellowed. "Let's get out of here."

The lines of tracer wove closer and closer to their target. Another anti-aircraft shell exploded too near for comfort. Chalkie kept his eye on the target.
Not yet. Not yet.
Keep it steady. A metre either side, the bombs will go thumping into the fields.
Chalkie lined up the Mosquito for the final five-hundred-metre approach. Then, in disbelief, he and Mac saw men starting to run from the workshop.
There are CIVILIANS inside!
They're not supposed to be there. Our intelligence was that they started half an hour after dawn. What's going on?

Four hundred metres!
Three hundred!
TWO HUNDRED!

Chalkie had to make a split-second decision – release almost a tonne of high explosive onto the innocent civilians – or put himself and his navigator in mortal danger.

"Go round!" yelled Mac, making it for him. "Go round!"

Chalkie hauled back on the control stick and the Mosquito soared skywards, shuddering under the strain of the urgent manoeuvre.

The site for the new school was deserted. A red warning ribbon, stretched around the entire area, kept the contractors and the other onlookers a hundred metres from the shallow hole where the digger operator had made his grim discovery. He'd been lucky. Another centimetre below, and the results could have been disastrous.

The army had been notified immediately, and an emergency team arrived at St Augiére within hours. After inspecting the grey, rusting object, the army officer knew exactly what he had to do. He dialled a number and notified his commander.

"UXB," he said grimly. "An unexploded bomb, and it appears old and dangerously corroded." He'd heard of these before. With thousands of bombs dropped over his country during the war, hundreds had failed to detonate. Forty years later, they remained beneath the surface, slowly rusting, their detonation fuses becoming more and more unstable. Building works usually uncovered them. Luckily, this building crew had been smart enough to abandon their site at once. Others hadn't. Ignorant of the risk, they often continued digging around the strange cylinders they found metres beneath the ground, putting themselves and the surrounding area in terrible danger.

"I'll alert the bomb disposal unit," replied the commander. "Clear the area and don't disturb a thing until the Département du Déminage *arrive."*

4 Shot Down!

The German troops flung themselves to the ground as the Mosquito thundered overhead, mere metres above the workshop. The roar of its straining engines was deafening, drowning out the desperate shouts of the men still trapped inside the workshop.

The wooded slopes at the head of the valley rose up to meet Chalkie at alarming speed. With every fibre of his body, he willed the aircraft to climb. The Mosquito missed the tips of the trees with centimetres to spare, and Chalkie pulled his aircraft into a wide turn, exposing his full profile to the gunners below.

"Fire!" screamed the anti-aircraft commander furiously, ordering his troops up from where they'd thrown themselves on the ground. He jabbed a furious finger at the Mosquito, executing a painfully slow turn above the forest behind them. "Fire!" he yelled again.

At last, Sebastian and Roland squeezed themselves through the steel door and ran as fast as they could. They'd heard the bellowing engines overhead and waited, terrified, for the blast – but for some reason, there was nothing. What was going on? Had the bombs they expected missed and failed to detonate?

"This is not going to be good," said Chalkie grimly, as he flew back along the ridge of the valley, then dropped down in a low, curving swoop. Both men knew that, with the Germans fully prepared and waiting for them, a second bombing run would be almost suicidal. The pilot steadied his aircraft and pushed the throttle full ahead once more.

"Second time lucky," remarked Mac.

"It will be for those men inside the workshop," said Chalkie grimly. "But not for us."

Behind the cordon, one member of the bomb disposal team donned a huge padded suit, while another soldier helped him secure his blast-proof headgear.

"You're all set, Jean-Claude," said the second soldier, giving the thumbs-up sign.

Jean-Claude headed slowly towards the abandoned digger. Lying on his stomach, he inched towards the hole and peered inside. Jean-Claude gently brushed some soil away from the UXB, looking for identifying marks. Fortunately, the UXB had come to rest with its detonation fuse facing upright, which meant at least they wouldn't have the dangerous and painstaking task of digging beneath the bomb to defuse it. He examined the rusting, corroded area carefully, then pushed himself backwards. He stood up and lumbered back to his team.

"Four-fifty kilo, British, usual corrosion for a wartime UXB. Looks like a delayed detonation fuse, not an impact detonation fuse, which means it could be live," reported Jean-Claude. "With an impact detonation fuse, there's a good chance the explosive was faulty. Unfortunately, with a delayed detonation fuse,

there's no telling. The explosive could still be live, and the detonation fuse trigger might just need a nudge to set it off."

"I'll get an engineer to bring us a wiring diagram," said one of the bomb disposal team. "We've got all the British detonation fuses on file."

There was a commotion behind them, as a tall man pushed his way through the crowd of contractors.

"What's going on here?" he demanded.

"Who are you?" asked Jean-Claude politely.

"I'm the mayor," snapped the man, drawing himself up to his full height and fixing the soldier with cold, grey, expressionless eyes. "Why are these workers standing around and why are the trenches for my school's foundations not being completed?"

"I'm afraid, Monsieur Mayor, that there will be a delay in your project," replied Jean-Claude. "St Augiére is lucky it doesn't have a gigantic crater instead of a trench."

Five hundred metres out, Chalkie knew his Mosquito was doomed. They'd lost the element of surprise and the German gunners were prepared and determined, their bullets and shells finding their target relentlessly. One of his engines had exploded into flames and the Mosquito was shuddering violently, shaking itself to bits. Four hundred. Three hundred. Chalkie fought desperately to keep the mortally wounded aircraft on track.

"Not yet. Not yet," he grimaced, checking there were now no more civilians escaping the workshop. Two hundred metres. One hundred.

"NOW!" came Mac's voice.

"Bombs away!" he called and at that exact moment, his cockpit windscreen shattered into a thousand fragments.

"Chalkie, watch out!" came a warning yell from behind him. Free from its deadly load, the Mosquito lurched sideways, careering towards the forest beyond the target. With only one engine, the aircraft struggled to find the power to climb away from the looming trees.

A sickening thump tore through the air and the Mosquito's tail jolted upwards as if it had been kicked violently from below. Behind them, Chalkie knew that one of the bombs had exploded. With its tail forced upwards, the Mosquito now veered down towards the rapidly approaching trees.

A kilometre from the workshop, the left wing of the Mosquito smashed into a tall fir tree and was instantly torn off. The bomber careered sideways and dived into the forest.

His leg ached, but he ignored it. The moment he'd reached his stop, he'd hurried through the ticket barriers and headed home, telephoning everyone he thought could help, gleaning what meagre information he could. He'd contacted journalists, librarians and the French embassy. There wasn't much. He stared at the photograph again. The man was rich, though the source of his wealth was unknown – a property developer who had somehow bought his way through most of the town, and then bought his way into local government.

The ache in his leg burned once more. He'd never had any desire to return. He'd spent forty years trying to forget. Too many bad memories. But, after seeing the photograph, he knew he had to go back. He had a debt to repay. He zipped up the bag and headed outside.

He didn't have to wait long before a black cab drove down his street.

"Victoria Station," he said, climbing into the back seat. The cabbie did a U-turn and headed for the train station.

"Going on holiday?" asked the cabbie.

"Catching the train to Gatwick Airport," replied the passenger.

"Don't like flying," offered the cabbie, shaking his head. "Turbulence frightens me."

The passenger settled back in his seat. "Haven't been flying myself for quite a long time," he replied. "I'm sure it's become a lot safer over the years."

The cab driver concentrated on the road ahead while his passenger unzipped his bag and drew out the newspaper clipping. Those eyes. He'd never forget them.

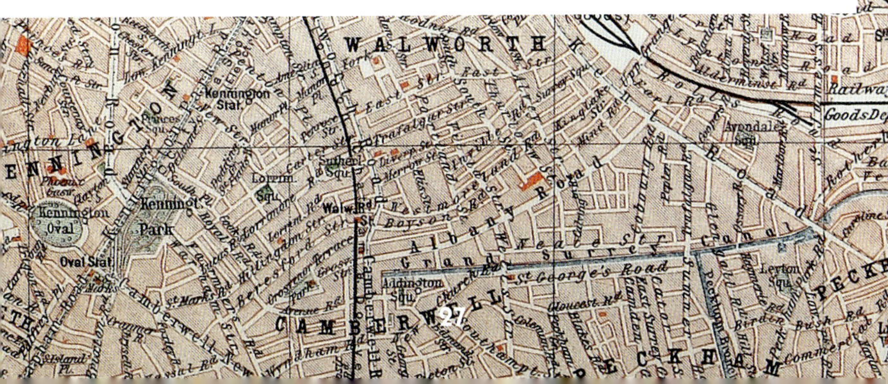

When Chalkie regained consciousness, he found himself still strapped into the wrecked cockpit. His first instinct was to twist himself around and check on Mac. Instantly, a searing pain shot through his left leg.

"Mac!" he whispered, gritting his teeth. "Mac! Are you OK?"

Mac groaned, and Chalkie breathed a sigh of relief. At least he was still alive. Chalkie looked around the crash site. Smouldering pieces of wreckage lay everywhere, strewn throughout the trees, but miraculously, the fuselage had stayed intact. That's what had saved them.

"Come on, Mac, we've got to get out," he croaked. Chalkie unclipped his harness and, despite the shooting pains coming from his leg, pushed himself up out of his seat. He clambered to the edge of the cockpit and hauled himself over the edge, then fell to the ground, his wounded leg collapsing underneath him.

Mac groaned again. Chalkie struggled to his feet, putting all his weight on his good leg, and eventually managed to release Mac's safety harness. He pulled

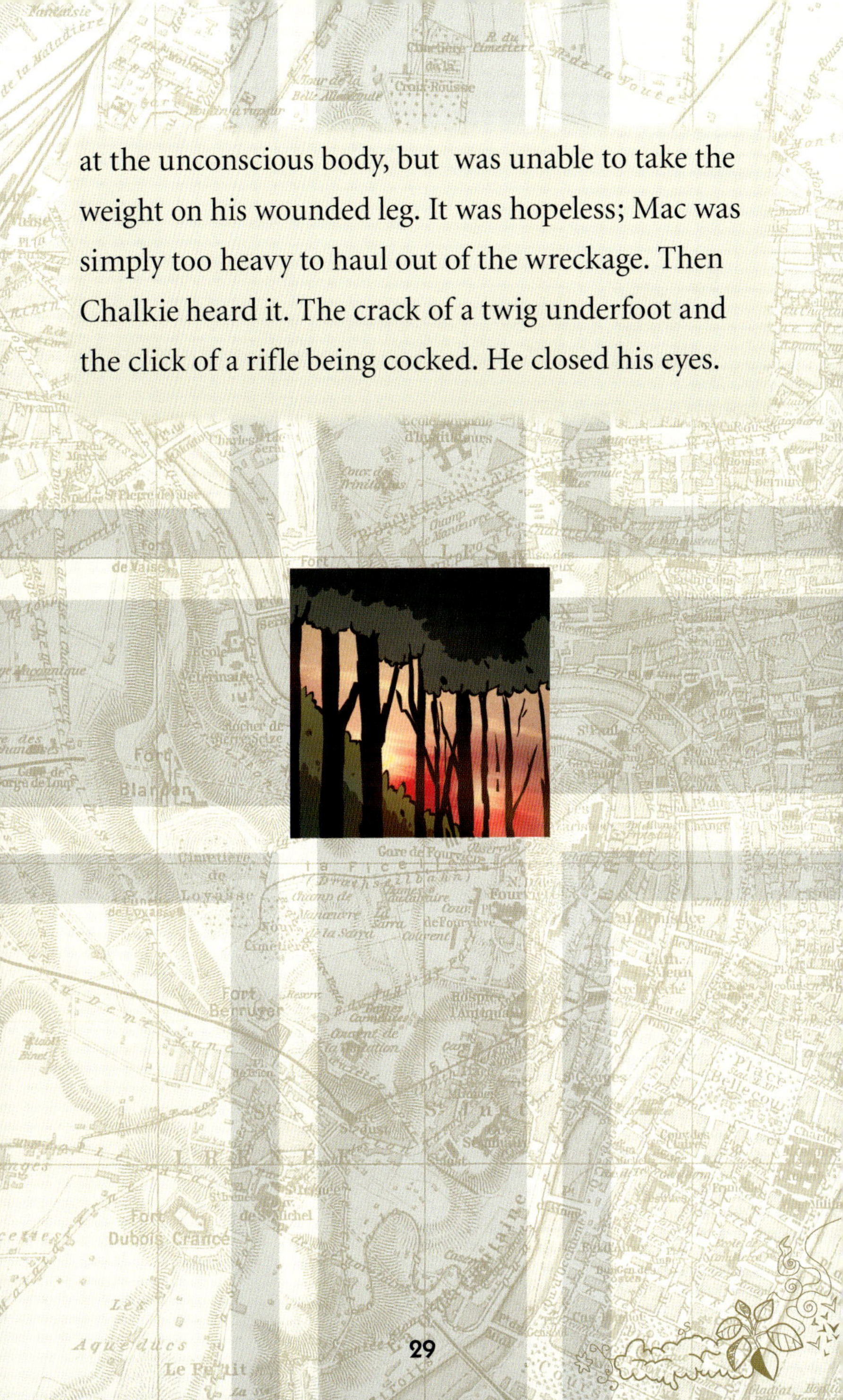

at the unconscious body, but was unable to take the weight on his wounded leg. It was hopeless; Mac was simply too heavy to haul out of the wreckage. Then Chalkie heard it. The crack of a twig underfoot and the click of a rifle being cocked. He closed his eyes.

5 A Rescue and Betrayal

"Are you British?" came a wary voice. Chalkie slowly hobbled around, his hands up. And then he gasped.

A young woman crouched between two trees, aiming a hunting rifle directly at Chalkie.

"Are you British?" she repeated, her finger on the trigger.

Chalkie nodded. He wasn't sure what was happening, but at least she wasn't a German soldier, he thought.

The young woman kept the rifle trained on Chalkie and eyed him suspiciously. "Is your friend still alive?" she asked, nodding at Mac.

???

Is your friend still alive?

"Local authorities say work on a new school has been halted in the small French town of St Augiére due to the discovery of an unexploded World War II bomb during excavation. Around 900 tonnes of unexploded munitions are found in France every year. The French bomb disposal unit, the Département du Déminage, *say that the discovery is in a remote area of France not thought to have been the subject of significant action, and is a timely reminder that all unidentified buried objects should be treated with caution. The mayor of St Augiére says disposal is expected to be completed within a week."*

"Not thought to have been the subject of significant action," read the man in the back seat of the black cab. He gazed out of the window. "It was significant for some," he thought.

After a week, Chalkie was able to hobble around the attic of the farmhouse. He still didn't know how they'd done it, he and the young woman. Her name was Monique and she despised the foreign soldiers who had invaded her country.

Together, they'd hauled Mac's unconscious body out of the wreckage and set fire to what remained of the Mosquito. With any luck, the Germans would think both men had been trapped inside and would give up their search for fugitive enemy aviators. Rough splints were tightly bandaged around Mac's broken ankle, and he rested on an old straw mattress, drifting in and out of consciousness, badly hurt. He needed help.

Chalkie heard footsteps climbing the stairs to the attic.

"Here, drink this," said Monique, offering him a bowl of thin soup. She looked at Mac. "I have some friends in the village who are in contact with people – members of the resistance. They will come soon and take you and your friend somewhere safer."

Chalkie nodded and smiled at Monique.

He knew the terrible risk she was taking by hiding them. If the Germans found them, he and Mac would end up as prisoners – but there would be more terrible consequences for Monique and her family. Harbouring the Germans' enemies was very, very dangerous. But Monique was brave and had not hesitated for a second.

On the ground, nothing looked the same. A shopping centre dominated the centre of the small town. A new property development sprawled up a hillside, where once there had been nothing but forest. The visitor to St Augiére wondered, for a moment, if forty years had blurred his memory too much. Perhaps he had made a mistake. He recognised nothing – until he turned a corner and saw the old engineering works.

The rail tracks leading to the workshop were disused and overgrown, and on the building itself was a real estate agent's sign. It looked smaller than he remembered, and what he had failed to achieve all those years ago, time and disrepair had accomplished. The building was a ruin.

The visitor peered at the sign. "New holiday apartment complex coming soon. Register your interest now," it read.

The visitor saw the red, flapping tape of the cordon around the building site next door to the old workshop and walked over to join the people who were watching the bomb unit's progress from a safe distance.

Chalkie heard the sound of raised voices below the attic floor. Monique and her father, Sebastian, were arguing with the youngest member of the family, Roland. The moment he'd laid eyes on the fighter pilot and navigator, Chalkie knew that, in Roland's eyes, they were a risk not worth taking.

"They can't stay here," came Roland's heated voice through the floorboards. "You know what the Germans will do if they discover we are harbouring enemy aircrew."

"They are not enemy aircrew," retorted Monique. "They are British aircrew. And you are alive today thanks to their bravery, because if they'd dropped their bombs on their first run, you wouldn't be here now, acting like a spoilt child."

If the Germans find them, it'll be my life on the line, too.
A few more days, Roland, and they'll be gone.
SLAM!
Chalkie knew what he had to do. He couldn't risk the lives of the young woman and her family any longer.

"She's right," came Sebastian's voice. "Those men spared our lives, and we should help save theirs."

"You're mad," replied Roland. "You can endanger your lives all you want, but not mine. If the Germans find them, it'll be my life on the line, too."

"A few more days, Roland, and they'll be gone," said Monique. There was a scraping of chairs, and then a door slammed.

Chalkie knew what he had to do. He couldn't risk the lives of the young woman and her family any longer. He'd ask Monique and her father to help them down to a nearby road that night, where he and Mac would wait until they were discovered in the morning. He'd say they'd been evading capture in the forest and no one would ever know about Monique and Sebastian.

The mayor of St Augiére was annoyed. He was used to getting his way. The shopping centre, the housing development, the apartment complex – there'd been objections to them all, but he'd managed to avoid delays. Now, the one thing he was doing that wouldn't make him any money was also delayed. He'd have to reschedule the foundation ceremony until Friday because of that wretched old bomb.

The phone on his desk rang. "Oui?" *he answered. There was a brief conversation, and the mayor put down the phone. The* Département du Déminage *had dealt with the old UXB sooner than expected. It had been defused and they were awaiting a crane truck to remove it to a safe area for controlled detonation. He returned to his speech. He wanted to make sure it was a good one. He had, after all, ensured that the school had been named after him, in recognition of his sterling work as a local business operator and benefactor.*

He wouldn't reschedule; he would do it while they were removing the old bomb in the background. It would be great theatre and local politicians loved great theatre. It ensured they made the coveted front pages of the local, and maybe even national, newspapers.

Chalkie sat on the edge of Mac's mattress, pondering his fate. He'd be a prisoner for the rest of the war, but he'd manage. And, as a prisoner too, Mac would at least get the medical help he desperately needed. It had to be done, decided Chalkie, knowing there was no other option.

He heard the door downstairs again and more scraping of chairs, followed by the sound of footsteps on the stairs. Monique would be bringing some bread or tea. He'd tell her, and that night this dangerous situation would be resolved. He heard another set of footsteps coming up the stairs. That would be Sebastian. Good. He could explain his plan to them both.

Then he heard more footsteps. Roland? Well, he'd be pleased they were giving themselves up, no doubt. And then Chalkie's heart missed a beat. The stairs creaked as more and more footsteps crept towards the attic. Who else was there? Members of the resistance?

BETRAYAL!
There he is! That's him!
Hands up, Britisher!
How could you?

Suddenly, the door to the attic crashed inwards and Chalkie's blood ran cold. In horror, he saw Roland, pointing, while crowded behind him stood a squad of German soldiers in grey uniforms, with guns at the ready.

The men rushed past Roland, into the attic. Chalkie raised his hands, never for a moment taking his eyes off Roland, who returned his gaze with cold, expressionless eyes.

Disbelief and anger flooded his body. Roland had betrayed not only him and Mac, but his sister and father.

"How could you?" whispered Chalkie in shock.

6 Another UXB Awaits

"Just one night," explained the visitor to the manager of the guesthouse. "I just need a room for one night."

The manager showed him to his room, and the visitor lay down wearily on his bed. He'd been walking around all day and his leg was aching. He was also disappointed. He didn't know what he expected, but nothing about the small town was as he remembered. He hadn't even been able to locate the old farmhouse, which had disappeared, replaced by ugly post-war housing. He wondered if some things were better forgotten. The events of the past were buried, like some rusting old munitions from long ago. Disturbing them, as the contractors at the school site had discovered, could only cause trouble.

He'd gone to the municipal offices but couldn't bring himself to walk up the steps. He wasn't sure if he could do this. What would he say? Who would believe him? And then he saw the notice, displayed on the municipal noticeboard. A foundation ceremony. Once again, the face he despised stared out at him.

A group of townspeople had gathered near the site of the new school. A local TV camera operator was there, and a newspaper reporter was taking photos. A light crane was working in the background, but the crowd's focus was on a tall man who was speaking from a raised platform.

"As your mayor, I am proud to have been the driving force behind this development, which will soon become our new school. A school, I am humbled to say, which will bear my illustrious name."

The visitor moved closer and closer, pushing his way through the small gathering until he stood in front of everyone else, shoulder to shoulder with the TV camera operator and the newspaper reporter.

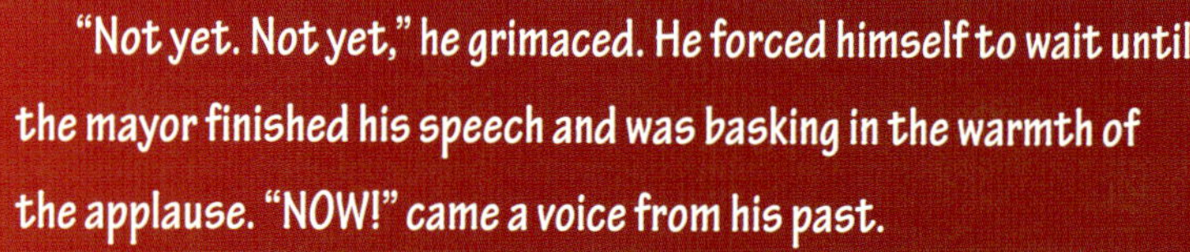

"Not yet. Not yet," he grimaced. He forced himself to wait until the mayor finished his speech and was basking in the warmth of the applause. "NOW!" came a voice from his past.

"Monsieur Mayor!" he called loudly, so everyone could hear. "I dropped two bombs on St Augiére that morning, forty years ago."

NOW!

Surely not?

Behind him, the crowd fell silent. The mayor glared. Who dared interrupt his moment of glory?
"One exploded. The other you have just defused."
The mayor peered closer. His blood ran cold. Surely not?
But another UXB remains in St Augiére.
That UXB is the truth about you and your long-buried betrayals.
It seems that truth has lain hidden, deep beneath the surface for forty years, but the damning explosive it contains is still very much alive.

The crowd gasped, and the TV camera operator and newspaper reporter switched their attention to the stranger standing next to them.

The mayor was confused. "Well then, call the bomb squad," he said in a shaky voice.

"It's too late, Roland," said Chalkie. "This UXB also has a delayed detonation fuse. Much too delayed."

Roland's mouth opened and closed. This couldn't be happening.

"But I can assure you that delayed detonation fuse was definitely triggered," said Chalkie, staring with his own cold, expressionless eyes at the man who'd betrayed his own family and country forty years ago. "And, believe me, in ten minutes, when I've told my story to the newspaper reporters, the TV crews and the people gathered here today from this village, that UXB will detonate underneath you."

UXB!